GOOD KING WENCESLAS

Pauline Baynes

Lutterworth Press
Cambridge

GOOD KING WENCESLAS

Piae Cantiones, 1582

1 Good King Wenceslas looked out
   On the Feast of Stephen,
When the snow lay round about,
   Deep and crisp and even:
Brightly shone the moon that night,
   Though the frost was cruel,
When a poor man came in sight
   Gathering winter fuel.

2 'Hither, page, and stand by me,
   If thou know'st it, telling,
Yonder peasant, who is he?
   Where and what his dwelling?'
'Sire, he lives a good league hence,
   Underneath the mountain,
Right against the forest fence,
   By Saint Agnes' fountain.'

3 'Bring me flesh, and bring me wine,
   Bring me pine-logs hither:
Thou and I will see him dine,
   When we bear them thither.'
Page and monarch, forth they went,
   Forth they went together;
Through the rude wind's wild lament
   And the bitter weather.

4 'Sire, the night is darker now,
   And the wind blows stronger;
Fails my heart, I know not how;
   I can go no longer.'
'Mark my footsteps, good my page;
   Tread thou in them boldly:
Thou shalt find the winter's rage
   Freeze thy blood less coldly.'

5 In his master's steps he trod,
   Where the snow lay dinted;
Heat was in the very sod
   Which the Saint had printed.
Therefore, Christian men, be sure,
   Wealth or rank possessing,
Ye who now will bless the poor,
   Shall yourselves find blessing.

J. M. Neale (1818–1866)

THE STORY OF
GOOD KING WENCESLAS

Many years ago two young princes lived in Bohemia. They were called Wenceslas and Boleslav. They lived in times of violence, when arguments were usually settled by bloodshed and battles.

When Wenceslas was nine years old his father died. His mother now ruled the country. She was a cruel and ruthless woman. She had no time for Wenceslas, and sent him to live with his grandmother, the old Queen Ludmilla, but she kept her younger son, Boleslav, with her.

Queen Ludmilla, unlike most people in those wild days, was a devout Christian, and a good and holy woman. She loved her grandson Wenceslas, and taught him to be a Christian like herself. When Wenceslas' mother, who was not a Christian, heard that her son was being brought up more like a gentle priest than a fierce and strong king, she was furious. She summoned Wenceslas home, and in her anger banished Queen Ludmilla from the country, and then arranged for her to be killed.

Back home with his mother and brother, Wenceslas refused to give up his Christian beliefs. The more his mother tried to persuade him to forget what his grandmother had taught him, the more devout he became. He also taught himself to read and write, rare skills in those days, so that he could read the Bible for himself. He arranged for priests to be smuggled into the castle at night so that he could learn more from them.

Wenceslas was brave as well as resolute. At the age of fourteen he rode at the head of an army sent to defeat the Duke of Bavaria who had invaded his country. People all over Bohemia recognised his authority and courage. They rallied round him so that by the time he was eighteen he was able to seize power from his mother who was too cruel to be a popular ruler.

There are many stories of his kindness. One tells of how Wenceslas trudged through deep snow for many miles with his faithful page Poidevin, to deliver food to a peasant who had been cut off by the snowdrifts. It was said that Poidevin, though barefoot, felt no cold if he stepped in his master's footsteps.

Another legend tells of how Wenceslas used to creep out of his castle at night to cut wood from his own forests for the poor people. His forester reported that the trees were disappearing mysteriously, and asked for advice. The king told him to catch the thief if he could, and thrash him, but on no account to take the logs away from him. A few nights later Wenceslas was caught, and unrecognised in the dark, was duly thrashed. Nevertheless, he still delivered the firewood to the peasants.

Wenceslas knew how much suffering can be caused by war, and tried to spare his people whenever possible. On one expedition with his troops he met with a marauding army from a nearby country. In order to avoid bloodshed he offered to fight the leader in single combat. The challenge was accepted. Wenceslas won the duel, and the invading army retreated.

On another occasion the king of Saxony invaded Bohemia. He had a huge army, far outnumbering that of Wenceslas. Rather than have his entire army massacred, Wenceslas offered to come to terms. He agreed to pay a yearly tribute to Saxony of 500 pieces of silver and 120 oxen.

However, not everyone agreed that Wenceslas had acted wisely. Some saw his refusal to fight as weakness and as a defeat for Bohemia. Now his enemies took this opportunity to plot against him. His younger brother Boleslav had never become a Christian, and some of the nobles who were not Christian planned to place him on the throne instead of Wenceslas. Boleslav readily agreed to their scheme, and they plotted to get Wenceslas on his own.

So when Wenceslas received an invitation from Boleslav to open a new chapel he was delighted. He believed his brother had become a Christian at last. He and Poidevin set out unarmed. But, when they found the chapel, it was locked and deserted. As they turned to go, Boleslav suddenly appeared, sword in hand.

He struck Wenceslas a massive blow on the head, half-shattering his skull. When no blood came from the wound Boleslav screamed with terror. The other conspirators rushed in, swords and daggers in their hands, raining down blows on Wenceslas who was hacked to pieces. The brave Poidevin was able to kill one of his master's attackers, but was later hanged for his courageous action.

Wenceslas was only twenty-two years old when he was killed. His reign was brief, lasting only four years, but with his Christian ideals and his unselfish way of life he achieved so much that he has never been forgotten.

To this day we sing the carol at Christmas time, and remember him trudging through the snow, with the bitter wind whistling around him, the faithful Poidevin behind him, carrying gifts to the poor.

He was, indeed, a really *good* king.

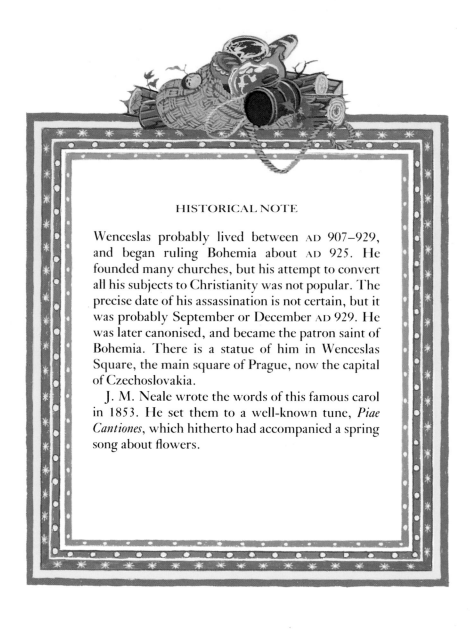

HISTORICAL NOTE

Wenceslas probably lived between AD 907–929, and began ruling Bohemia about AD 925. He founded many churches, but his attempt to convert all his subjects to Christianity was not popular. The precise date of his assassination is not certain, but it was probably September or December AD 929. He was later canonised, and became the patron saint of Bohemia. There is a statue of him in Wenceslas Square, the main square of Prague, now the capital of Czechoslovakia.

J. M. Neale wrote the words of this famous carol in 1853. He set them to a well-known tune, *Piae Cantiones*, which hitherto had accompanied a spring song about flowers.